# That Goat Must Go!

Story by Diana Noonan
Illustrations by Valentina Jaski[illegible]

## Contents

# Chapter 1

# A New Pet

Jordan loved pets.
He had a cat, a dog, two rabbits
and four hens.

What he wanted next was a goat.

"A goat could be a friend for my dog,"
said Jordan to his sister, Abby.

It was Jordan's birthday next week.

Jordan's uncle lived on a farm
with lots of goats.

"Maybe Uncle Pete could give me a goat
for my birthday," Jordan said to Mum.

"Let's wait and see," said Mum.

The next week, Uncle Pete drove to Jordan's birthday party in his truck.

In the back of the truck was a goat in a goat pen.

"Happy birthday, Jordan!" said Uncle Pete.

# Chapter 2

## A Goat in the Garden

Jordan named his goat Ginger.

That night, Jordan put Ginger in her pen
in the garden.
"This is your new home," he said, smiling.

In the morning,
Jordan woke up to a shout from Dad.

"Ginger ate all my roses!" Dad cried.
"That goat must go!"

"Wait!" said Jordan.
"I'll put her pen beside the tree."

But the next morning,
all the grass in Ginger's pen was gone.
And Mum's socks were gone, too!

"That goat must go!" shouted Mum.

"Wait!" said Jordan.
"I'll put Ginger's pen beside the house."

But the next morning,
all of Abby's pot plants were gone.

"That goat must go!" cried Abby.

# Chapter 3

# A New Place for Ginger

Meg lived next door to Jordan
and his family.

"I'll put Ginger beside Meg's fence,"
said Jordan.

But in the morning,
the blackberry plant in Meg's garden
had a big hole in it!

"That goat must go *now*!"
shouted Mum, Dad and Abby, all at once.

Meg looked over the fence from next door.
"No, that goat must stay!" she said, smiling.
"I need her to eat the blackberry plants."

"Can Ginger live in your garden?"
asked Jordan.

"Yes!" said Meg.
"As long as you move her to a new spot
in the garden every day."

So, Jordan moved Ginger's pen every day.

Ginger ate the blackberry plants
and the grass in Meg's garden.

"We like having Ginger next door," said Mum, Dad and Abby.

"So do I. And so does Ginger!" said Jordan.